**To every song that inspires me, to every child I hope to inspire, and to my family, who never stops loving and inspiring me every day (my mom, Danny, Soul Rebel, Skip, Saiyen, Lee, Molly, Oscar, and Bobby)**
**—C.M.**

**Dedicated to Bryce Theophile**
**—T.B.**

**Even on the stormiest of days, remember that the sunshine is only ever a few steps away.**
**—T.R.**



Visit us on the Web! rhcbooks.com
Educators and librarians, for a variety of teaching tools, visit us at RHTeachersLibrarians.com

*Library of Congress Cataloging-in-Publication Data*
Names: Marley, Cedella, author. | Rose, Tiffany, illustrator.
Title: Marley and the family band / Cedella Marley with Tracey Baptiste ; illustrated by Tiffany Rose.
Description: First edition. | New York : Random House | Summary: "Marley and her siblings plan to put on a community concert after moving from Jamaica to Delaware, but when rain threatens to ruin the day, they learn the power of lending a helping hand." —Provided by publisher.
Identifiers: LCCN 2020045978 (print) | LCCN 2020045979 (ebook) | ISBN 978-0-593-30111-1 (hardcover) | ISBN 978-0-593-30112-8 (library binding) | ISBN 978-0-593-30113-5 (epub)
Subjects: CYAC: Bands (Music)—Fiction. | Brothers and sisters—Fiction. | Jamaican Americans—Fiction.
Classification: LCC PZ7.M34438 Mar 2020 (print) | LCC PZ7.M34438 (ebook) | DDC [E]—dc23

The artist created the illustrations with digital crayon and watercolor brushes from Tip Top Brushes, using the digital drawing app Procreate.

The text of this book is set in 14-point Meta Pro.

Interior design by Sarah Hokanson

MANUFACTURED IN CHINA
10 9 8 7 6 5 4 3 2 1 First Edition

# Marley and the Family Band

CEDELLA MARLEY
WITH TRACEY BAPTISTE

ILLUSTRATED BY
TIFFANY ROSE

Random House
New York

Tonight was Marley's big night! Concert night.
Moving from Jamaica to Delaware had meant leaving friends behind.

But tonight, Marley would make a whole neighborhood of new friends . . . and fans!

Unfortunately, the weather had other plans. Marley tapped her feet to the rhythm of raindrops, all the way down to the kitchen.

Her father was plucking his guitar. Her mother had her worried face on. Her sister, Jayde, had her bossy face on.

"The concert is off," Jayde said. "It's a storm."

Marley knew about storms. In Jamaica, hurricanes whipped across the island.

“Don’t fret,”
her father sang.
“After one time
is another.”

Marley’s little brothers trudged in.
Zayne climbed into their father’s lap.
Axel poured himself some cereal.

Marley wasn't ready to give up on the concert.

"Where are you going?" her mother asked.

"To the park," said Marley. "You can't fix a problem until you look at it up close."

Marley was hopeful. But the park was a mess.

Marley marched over to the stage. Axel picked his way through the muck. Zayne jumped into every puddle. Their boots were a squishing, splashing symphony.

"What if we hang umbrellas from the stage lights to cover everyone?" Marley said.

"Who has that many umbrellas?" Axel asked.

Marley looked back at their new neighborhood and smiled. "I know about storms," Marley said. "They make problems. If we help our neighbors with their storm problems, maybe . . ."

At the first house, they introduced themselves to Mrs. Harris. Her cat Coda had jumped on top of the garage when the thunder started.

Axel called softly while Zayne waved a treat. When Coda got close, Marley shooed her into a rain boot. For their help, Mrs. Harris gave them two umbrellas.

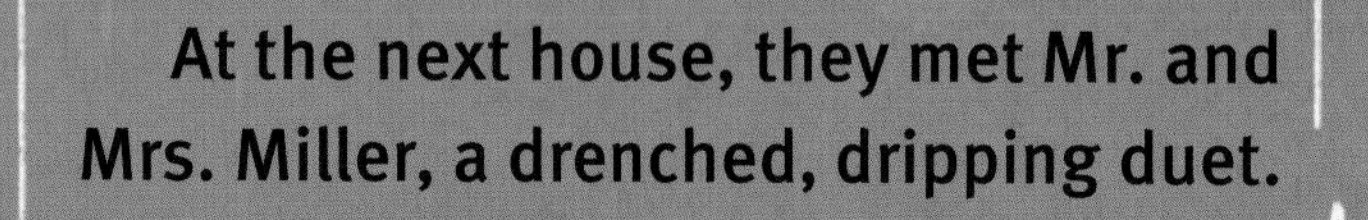

At the next house, they met Mr. and
Mrs. Miller, a drenched, dripping duet.

Marley, Axel, and Zayne helped bail water out of their basement.

The Millers happily gave them three bright umbrellas, plus a hat.

Next door, they found Mr. Canon, who had a broken leg. He needed their help picking basil and tomatoes from his greenhouse.

Thunder rattled the windows like cymbals. Mr. Canon gave them a big tarp.

Their neighbors seemed surprised at the problems caused by the rain. But Marley knew about storms.

Soon they had a tarp, eight umbrellas, and three rain hats.

At the last house, they heard screeching, meowing, barking, and squawking.

YAP-YAP-YAP!
MERROOOW!
CAAWW!
WOOOOFFFF!
CAAA-CAAAW!
ARF-ARF!
MEEOOOW!
MEOW!
HISSSS!

A young woman answered the door. Rain was coming in through a hole in the ceiling and pouring onto her many, many pets.

Marley looked at her umbrellas and her tarp. She looked at the wet pets. She knew the solution to *this* problem.

"Can we help you?"

There was a lot of squawking, mewing, hissing, barking, and bolting as Marley, Axel, and Zayne helped.

WHEEEK!
CAAW-CAAAW!
MEOW!
MEEER
MEEOOOW!
MEOW

“Tell me—what’s brought you all here?” the woman asked.

Marley explained. About their move. About the concert. About why they had so many umbrellas.

“I’m sorry I’ve ruined your plan,” the woman said.

Marley shrugged. “Rain never lasts.” She smiled. But it wasn’t a very sunny smile.

Back at home, their mother was on the phone. Their dad was strumming an upbeat tune.

"We're getting ready for the concert," Jayde said.
"But it's still raining," Marley said.
"Your friends solved that problem," said their mother.
"What friends?" Marley asked.
"All the people you helped today."

It was dry in Mr. Canon's greenhouse that night. Lightning lit up the space where Marley and her family would perform.

MARLEY AND
THE FAMILY BAND

Toes tapped inside rain boots. Thunder came in with some bass. Rain plinked on the glass. The concert jammed.

Marley and the family band were a big splash!